FOR **THE TRIXTER,**
MY OWN LITTLE MONSTER

WALKER BOOKS
AND SUBSIDIARIES
LONDON · BOSTON · SYDNEY · AUCKLAND

This edition published in Great Britain 2007
by Walker Books Ltd, 87 Vauxhall Walk, London SE11 5HJ

10 9 8 7 6 5 4 3 2 1

© 2005 Mo Willems

The right of Mo Willems to be identified as author/illustrator of this work
has been asserted by him in accordance with the Copyright, Designs and
Patents Act 1988

First published in the United States 2005 by Hyperion Books for Children.
British publication rights arranged with Sheldon Fogelman Agency, Inc.

This book has been typeset in Extravaganza

Printed in China

British Library Cataloguing in Publication Data:
a catalogue record for this book is available from the British Library

ISBN 978-1-4063-0807-5 (HB)
ISBN 978-1-4063-1215-7 (PB)

www.walkerbooks.co.uk

YOUR PAL MO WILLEMS PRESENTS

Leonardo the TERRIBLE MONSTER

WALKER BOOKS

LEONARDO

WAS A

TERRIBLE

MONSTER...

HE COULDN'T SCARE ANYONE.

HE DIDN'T HAVE 1,642* TEETH, LIKE TONY.

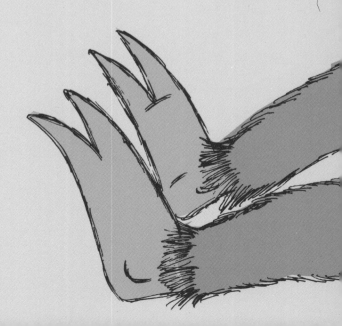

*NOTE: NOT ALL TEETH SHOWN.

HE
WASN'T
BIG,
LIKE
ELEANOR.

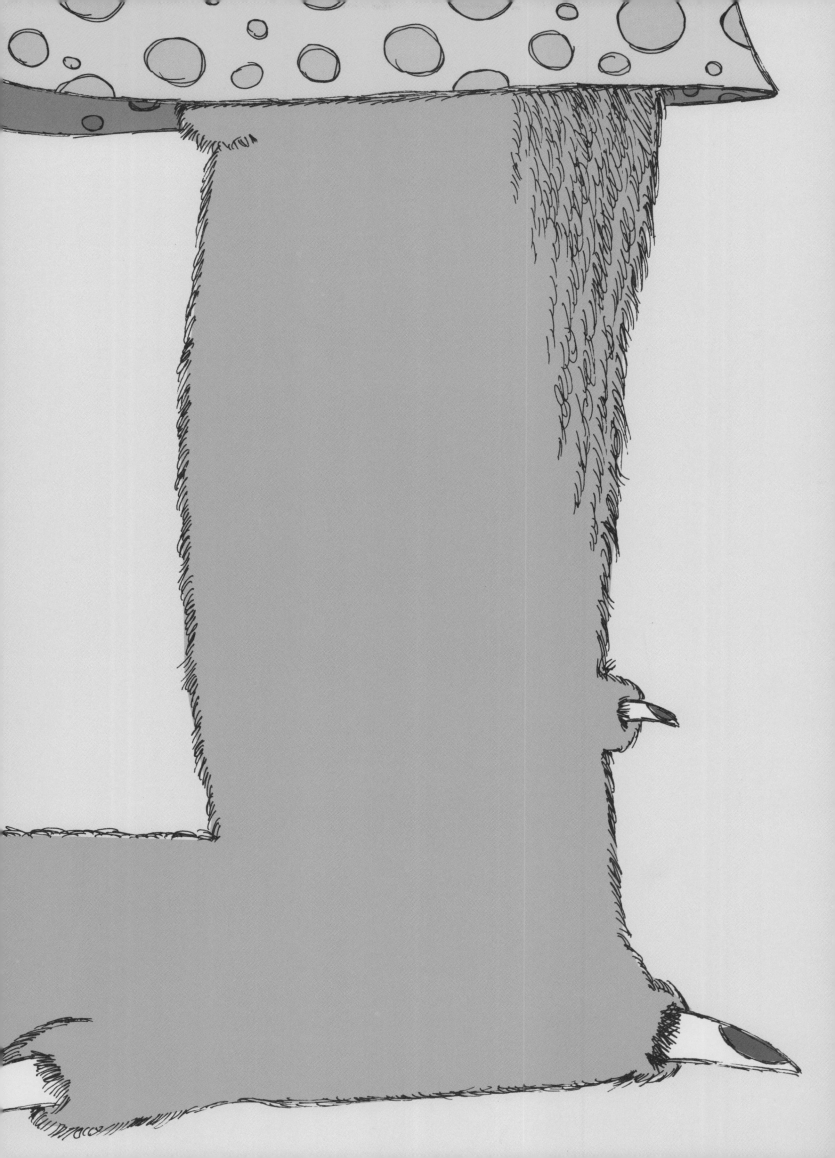

AND HE WASN'T
JUST PLAIN WEIRD,
LIKE HECTOR.

LEONARDO TRIED VERY HARD TO BE SCARY.

BUT...

HE JUST WASN'T.

ONE DAY,
LEONARDO HAD AN IDEA.
HE WOULD FIND THE MOST
SCAREDY-CAT KID IN
THE WHOLE WORLD...

AND SCARE THE TUNA SALAD OUT OF HIM!

LEONARDO RESEARCHED

UNTIL HE FOUND THE PERFECT CANDIDATE...

SAM.

LEONARDO SNUCK UP ON THE POOR, UNSUSPECTING BOY.

AND THE
MONSTER GAVE IT
ALL HE HAD.

UNTIL
THE LITTLE BOY
CRIED.

"YES!" CHEERED LEONARDO. "I DID IT! I'VE FINALLY SCARED THE TUNA SALAD OUT OF SOMEONE!"

"NO YOU DIDN'T!"
SNAPPED SAM.

"OH, YEAH?"
REPLIED
LEONARDO.
"THEN WHY
ARE YOU
CRYING?"

"MY MEAN BIG BROTHER STOLE

OF MY HANDS WHILE I WAS STILL

BROKE IT ON PURPOSE, AND I

TRIED TO FIX IT BUT I COULDN'T

TABLE AND I STUBBED MY TOE

LAST MONTH WHEN I ACCIDENTALLY

I GOT SOAP IN MY EYES TRYING TO

THAT MY BROTHER'S COCKATOO

DON'T HAVE ANY FRIENDS AND

MY ACTION FIGURE RIGHT OUT PLAYING WITH IT, AND THEN HE WAS MY FAVORITE TOY, AND I AND I GOT SO MAD I KICKED THE ON THE SAME FOOT THAT I HURT SLIPPED IN THE BATHTUB AFTER WASH OUT THE BIRD POO POOPED ON MY HEAD, AND I MY TUMMY HURTS!"

THEN
LEONARDO
MADE

A VERY BIG DECISION.